Rory and the Muncher Cruncher

written by
Jean Ball
Andrew Higgins

illustrated by
Genny Haines

Text © 2013 Andrew Higgins
Illustrations © 2013 Genny Haines

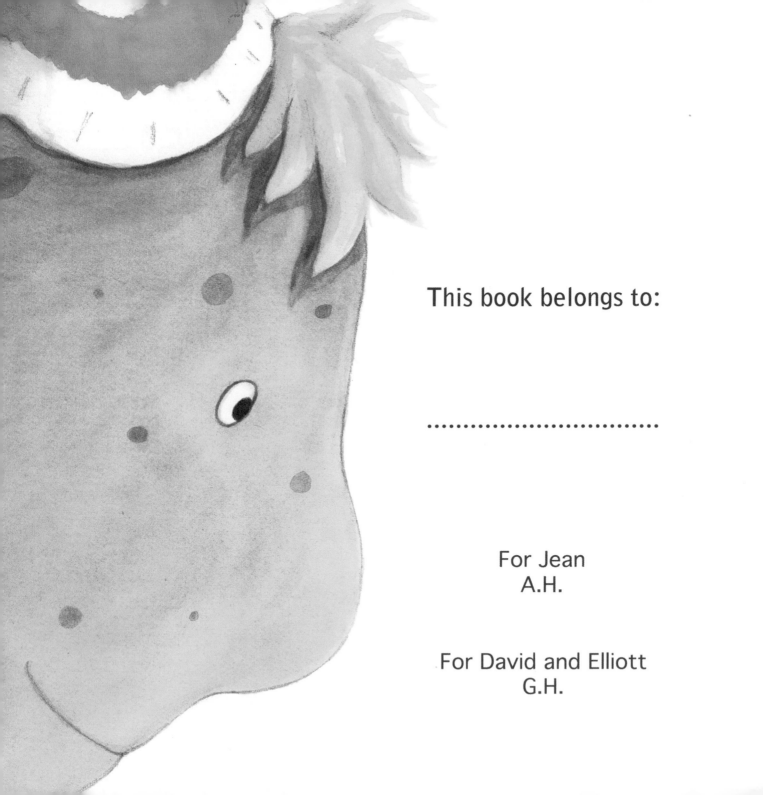

This book belongs to:

....

For Jean
A.H.

For David and Elliott
G.H.

Rory and the Muncher Cruncher

written by

Jean Ball

Andrew Higgins

illustrated by

Genny Haines

Rory had a **sweet** tooth.

Chocolate, cake, he loved everything sweet.

But his favourites were the **biscuits** his grandma made.

Every time Grandma visited, she **mixed, poured** and **baked...** and **Rory** did his best to help.

One night before bedtime Rory spotted something.

When nobody was watching he snuck the biscuits into his room.
As he was munching, Rory noticed that the cupboard door
was open.

He froze, as at night clothes could turn
into the monster **Muncher Cruncher!**
and if the cupboard wasn't closed...
there was nothing to stop it coming out!

Sure enough the door creaked
and winced and flew open with a *bang!*

Out sprang the **Muncher Cruncher**
landing, with a great **thump,** on Rory's bed.

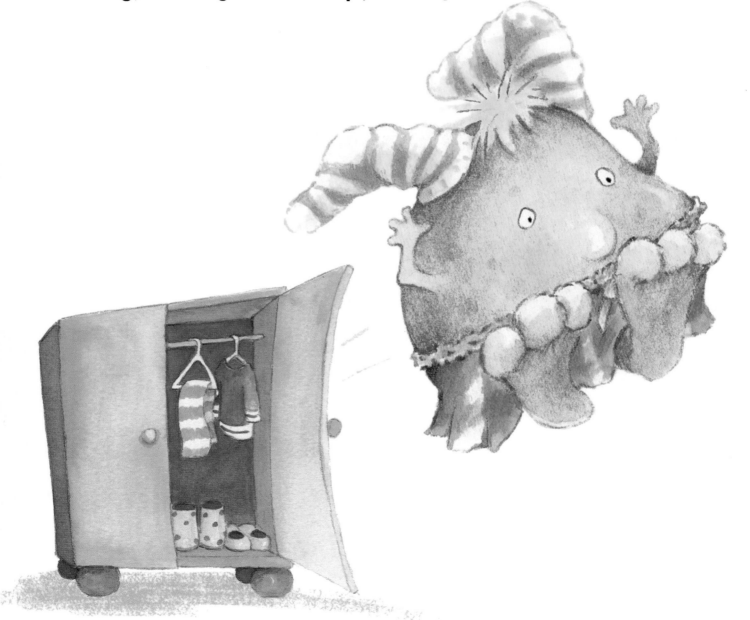

"**Yum!**" it said,
and **gobbled** up a biscuit.

Rory **bounced** off the bed...

and **hid.**

Trembling, **Rory** whispered,
"are you going to eat **me** too?"

But the **Muncher Cruncher** just looked at him, sighed deeply, clambered back onto the bed and waited and waited...

Eventually Rory **peeked** out from under the bed.
The Muncher Cruncher looked **sad.**

Carefully Rory put a biscuit in the muncher's hand.

"Yum," said the Muncher Cruncher.

"Yummy," said Rory.

And together they munched and crunched, until...

there were none left.

"We could make some more," said Rory,
"we don't have all the ingredients, but maybe we can buy them."

Rory had just enough pocket money.

"There's a store around the corner," said Rory,
"but the storeman won't sell to me, I should be in bed,
and he won't sell
to a monster."

The Muncher Cruncher put a **coat** and **hat** on Rory and
lifted him onto his head. "A disguise," said Rory, delighted.

But Rory couldn't remember where the **store** was.

They searched round this **corner,** then that **corner,** until...

there it was, around the **corner.**

They picked up the ingredients and Rory said to the store man,
"we'll buy **these** please".
The Muncher Cruncher was **SO** excited at the thought of eating
more biscuits his ears
let off a burst
of steam...

...and the coat **blew up** like a balloon.

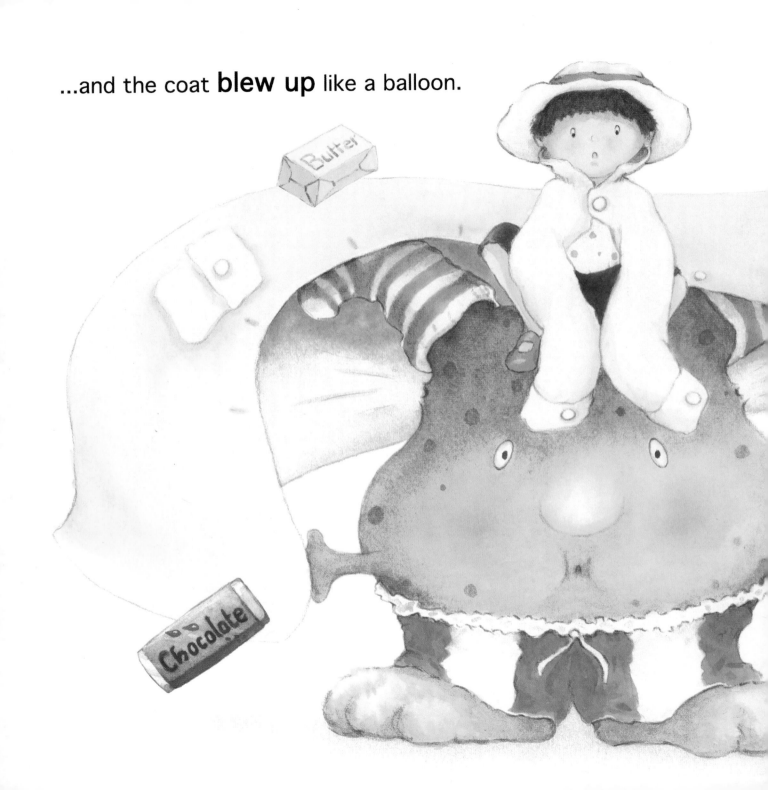

"What's going on?" said the store man.
"What have you got under that coat?"

'*Run!*'
cried Rory

and the monster ran...

...all the way home.

But back home they discovered
that the **chocolate** was **gone**.
They searched for some more.

"Nothing here,"
said Rory,

"Or in here."

They even looked in the **broom cupboard**.
To Rory's surprise, there in the corner was the **chocolate,**
tucked behind a **mouse!**

The Muncher Cruncher **jumped** in fright...
and Mouse **grabbed** the chocolate and took off.

Rory chased the **chocolate**
but **Mouse** was too quick.
He darted

this way

and that,

keeping just out of reach...

...until **chocolate**
and **Mouse** disappeared.

"Please return the chocolate, Mouse," whispered Rory, "we'll share the biscuits with you."

Mmmm... thought Mouse,
I do **like** biscuits.
And so the chocolate was returned.

Back in the kitchen they **measured** and **mixed** and added the **chocolate,**

greased the baking tray and poured the mixture.

Into the **oven** went the **biscuits**,
until they were **brown**
and crunchy.

They collected

them up and

...rushed back to Rory's bedroom...

and ate up every **biscuit**

until only

one

was left.

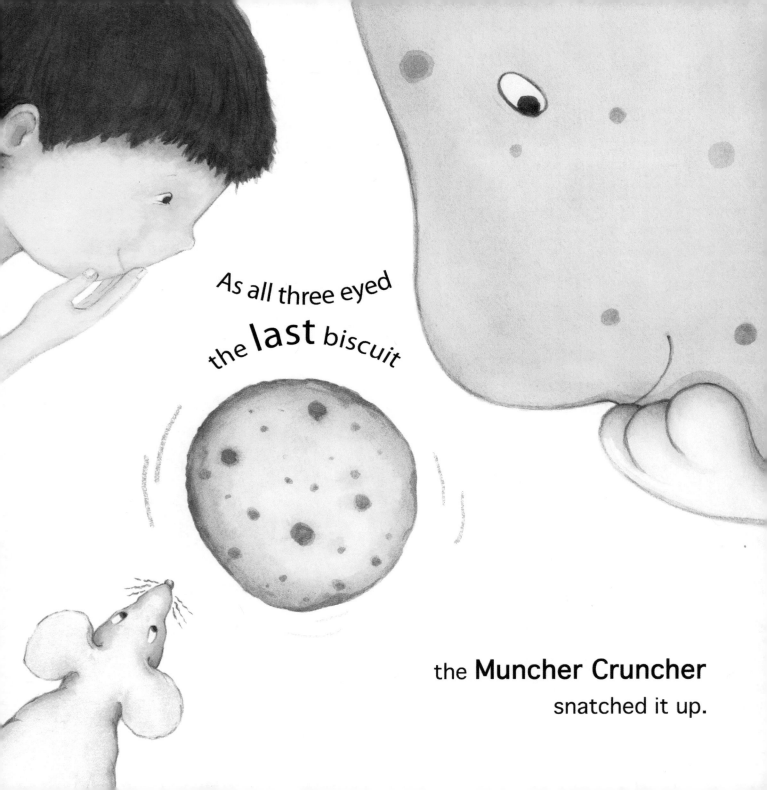

As all three eyed
the **last** biscuit

the **Muncher Cruncher**
snatched it up.

"Yum,"
said the Muncher Cruncher.
He lifted the biscuit up
to his mouth and...
SNAP!
broke it
into three.

With full tummies they settled down for the night.
The Muncher Cruncher left the cupboard door open
and Rory slept soundly.

The following morning
Rory leapt out of bed
to look for his
new friend.

No Muncher Cruncher could be seen,
but there was a faint munching sound.

When he looked closer, right at the back of the cupboard, he saw...

munch, munch,

crunch, crunch,

munch, munch...

"YUM!"

Made in the USA
San Bernardino, CA
29 April 2014